Old Meshikee AND THE Little Crabs

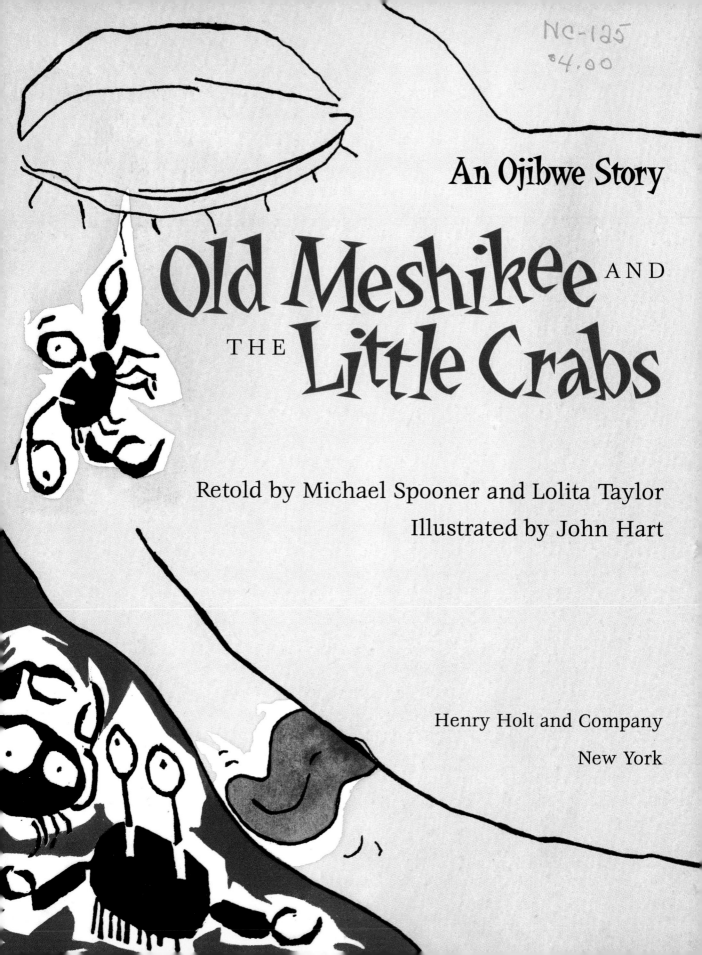

An Ojibwe Story

Old Meshikee AND THE Little Crabs

Retold by Michael Spooner and Lolita Taylor

Illustrated by John Hart

Henry Holt and Company

New York

Henry Holt and Company, Inc.
Publishers since 1866
115 West 18th Street
New York, New York 10011

Henry Holt is a registered
trademark of Henry Holt and Company, Inc.

Published in Canada by Fitzhenry & Whiteside Ltd.,
195 Allstate Parkway, Markham, Ontario L3R 4T8.

Library of Congress Cataloging-in-Publication Data
Spooner, Michael.
Old Meshikee and the little crabs: an Ojibwe story / retold by
Michael Spooner and Lolita Taylor; illustrated by John Hart.
Summary: Although the sand crabs try in many ways to get
rid of Old Meshikee the turtle, they are not as clever as he
and so fail to end his drumming.
1. Ojibwe Indians—Folklore. 2. Turtles—Great Lakes Region
—Folklore 3. Sand-crabs—Great Lakes Region—Folklore.
[Ojibwa Indians—Folklore. 2. Indians of North America—Folklore.
3. Folklore—North America.] I. Taylor, Lolita. II. Hart, John, ill.
III. Title.
E99.C6S737   1996   398.24'52792'089973—dcE   [20]   95-23498

ISBN 0-8050-3487-0

First Edition—1996

Printed in the United States of America on acid-free paper. ∞

10 9 8 7 6 5 4 3 2 1

The artist used a combination of watercolor and block printing
on etching paper to create the illustrations for this book.

ar in the north, near the Great Water of the Ojibwe people, Old Meshikee spends the summer on an island in the middle of a little lake. This lake is so beautiful and hidden so well that it doesn't even have a name. We'll call it Old Meshikee's Lake.

In the evening, the summer sun comes slanting late through the trees, and then the moon begins to rise above the water. And at this time of day, nothing makes Old Meshikee quite so happy as to sit beside his wigwam and make music for himself. The music that he plays is on his drum, of course. And since Old Meshikee is a big old turtle, he plays a big old drum, and what do you think his drum sounds like? It sounds loud, like this:

DRUMDRUM
DRUMDRUM
DRUMDRUM DRUMDRUM

On the shore of Old Meshikee's lake, across the water from his island, lives a whole village of little Shagizenz, or sand crabs. Now, the Shagizenz are industrious little animals, always building something, making something, always busy; not always too smart, however.

When they come to the end of a long day of working in the sand, the Shagizenz love to bring out their drums for some music and a dance. Of course, because they're small, the Shagizenz have very small drums, and even when there are many of these little drums, they make a rather small sound, something like this:

drumdrum drumdru$^m{}_m{}^m{}_m{}^m$
drumdrum drumdru$^m{}_m{}^m{}_m{}^m$

Not too loud, but it is enough for them, and they will sing their songs and dance happily all through the summer evening.

Unfortunately, it always seems to happen that just about the time the Shagizenz have their little drums going, and they are just beginning to have some fun,

drumdrum drumdru^m_mm

from across the water they hear Old Meshikee start up his evening songfest—

DRUMDRUM DRUMDRUMMM
DRUMDRUM DRUMDRUM_MM_M

—singing at the top of his lungs, and banging away on his big old drum. And always so loud the Shagizenz can scarcely hear their own music.

Many of the Shagizenz grow quite angry at this, and one day they decide that something must be done about Old Meshikee. So they call a council meeting in the big wigwam. When they come out of the meeting, the Shagizenz are clapping their hands and singing, "That's what we'll do! That's what we'll do!" and some of them are dragging a long rope they have made from the inside bark of an elm tree.

Very quietly, they push off in the biggest of their canoes and paddle across the lake to Old Meshikee's island. The day is warm, and when they arrive at the island, the Shagizenz are not surprised to find Old Meshikee dozing in the sun.

Quickly, quickly they tie up Old Meshikee with their rope and throw him roughly into the big canoe. When they reach their own shore again, the Shagizenz tumble Old Meshikee onto the yellow sand, where all their children play and make fun of him.

But what shall they do with Old Meshikee now that they have him? They gather in the big wigwam for another meeting.

Old Meshikee doesn't mind
the children teasing him; he teases them
right back and sticks out his tongue. But he wonders
what the Shagizenz are saying in their meeting. Old
Meshikee smiles. He has been alive a long, long time, and
he can almost guess what they'll do.

Now the Shagizenz are coming out of the big wigwam, very
pleased. "That's what we'll do! That's what we'll do!" they sing,
and they spread out immediately to gather wood for a fire. Some
pluck tiny dry twigs from the lowest branches of a pine tree,
some gather middle-size sticks from the forest, and the largest
of the Shagizenz run down the beach to drag an old gray
drift log to the fire. Old Meshikee smiles to himself,
but he makes his voice sound worried.

"What you gonna do?" he asks.
"What you gonna do?"

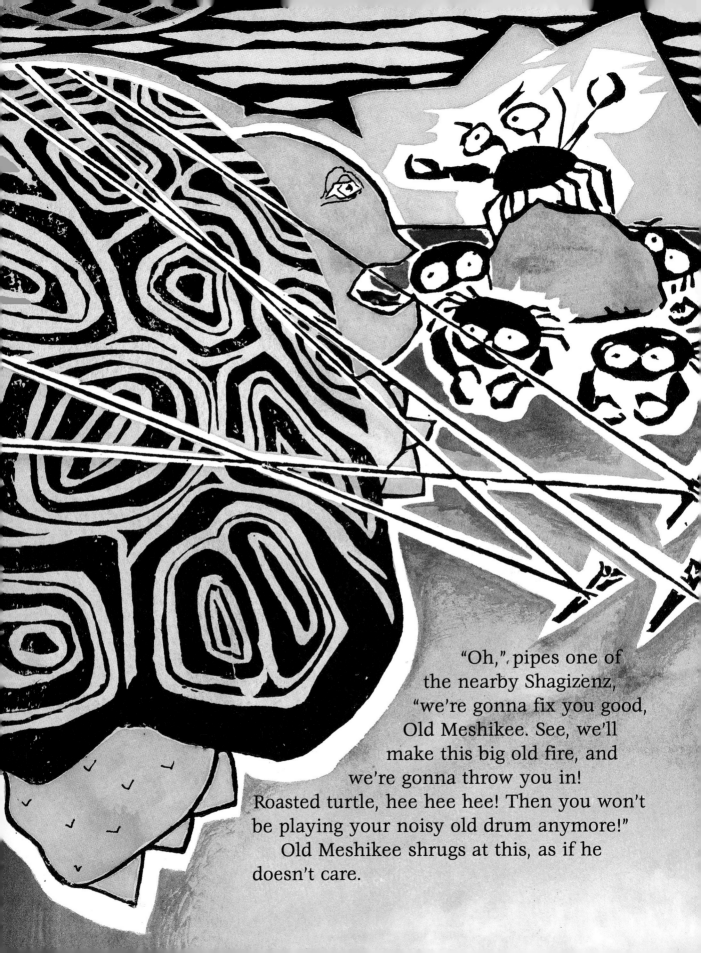

"Oh," pipes one of the nearby Shagizenz, "we're gonna fix you good, Old Meshikee. See, we'll make this big old fire, and we're gonna throw you in! Roasted turtle, hee hee hee! Then you won't be playing your noisy old drum anymore!"

Old Meshikee shrugs at this, as if he doesn't care.

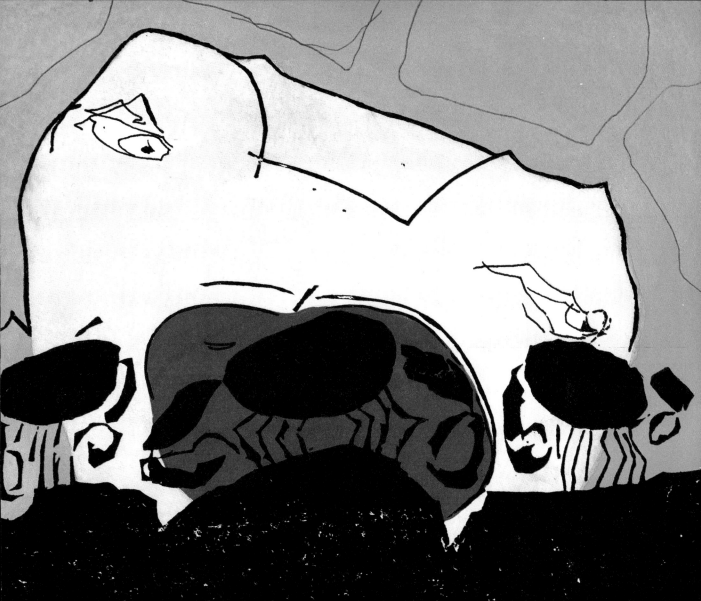

"Mah-jon, mah-jon," he says in a loud voice. "Throw me in your silly fire. But don't you know I'll thrash, and I'll kick, and all these burning sticks will scatter on your children?"

That makes the Shagizenz stop and think. "Hmmm," they say, looking at all the children digging in the yellow sand. "Can't do that. Can't do that."

"Anyway," says Old Meshikee, "I don't care about fire; it's only water that worries me."

So off go the Shagizenz to have another meeting. Old Meshikee begins to tease the Shagizenz children once again, asking them riddles that his grandfather taught him when he was a child.

The older Shagizenz don't take too long. They come out of the council meeting dragging an old iron kettle, and they are singing, "That's what we'll do! That's what we'll do!"

Some of the Shagizenz make a square crisscross of logs from the firewood and place the kettle on top of it. Others clatter down to the lake with baskets made of birch bark, which they dip full and carry back to the big iron kettle. Old Meshikee smiles to himself again, but he makes his voice sound worried.

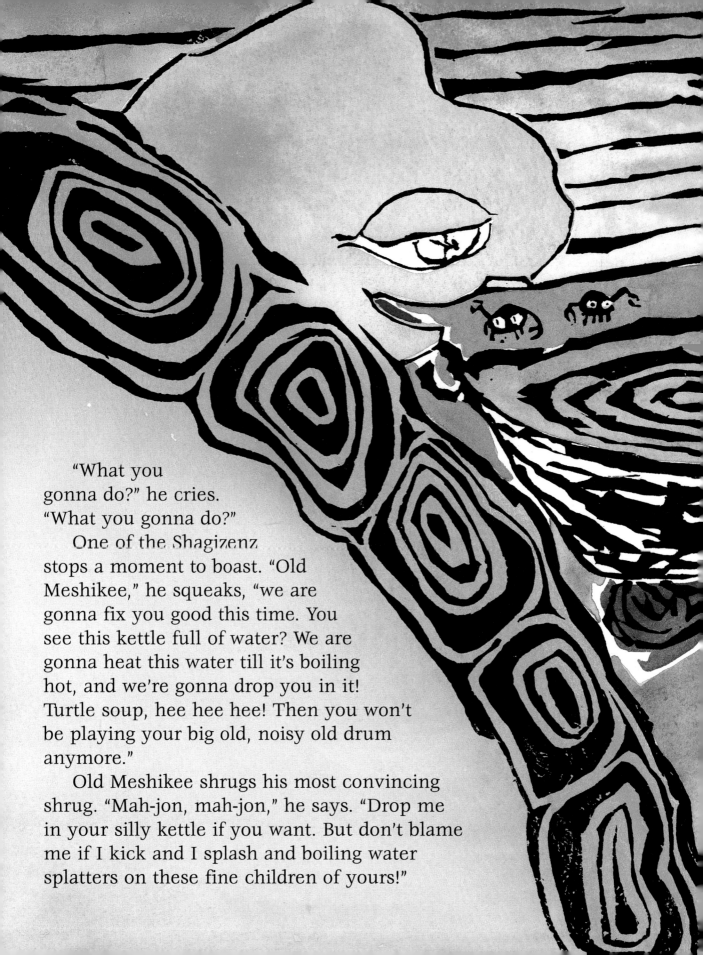

"What you
gonna do?" he cries.
"What you gonna do?"
   One of the Shagizenz
stops a moment to boast. "Old
Meshikee," he squeaks, "we are
gonna fix you good this time. You
see this kettle full of water? We are
gonna heat this water till it's boiling
hot, and we're gonna drop you in it!
Turtle soup, hee hee hee! Then you won't
be playing your big old, noisy old drum
anymore."
   Old Meshikee shrugs his most convincing
shrug. "Mah-jon, mah-jon," he says. "Drop me
in your silly kettle if you want. But don't blame
me if I kick and I splash and boiling water
splatters on these fine children of yours!"

Once again the Shagizenz have to stop and think. "Hmmm," they say, scratching their chins and counting the children who still play in the sand around Old Meshikee, around the kettle—in fact, all up and down the shore of the lake. How can there be so many of them? "Well," they grumble, "can't do that, can't do that."

"Anyway," says Old Meshikee, "I never cared about boiling water; it's the cold and deep that worries me."

Then off go the Shagizenz to have another meeting.

Old Meshikee shrugs. He turns back to the children of the Shagizenz gathered round, and begins to tell a story that his grandfather used to tell.

Soon come the older Shagizenz, marching out of the big wigwam. "That's what we'll do! That's what we'll do!" they are singing. Straightaway they push old Meshikee onto his back and begin to tie his legs.

"What you gonna do, little Shagizenz?" Old Meshikee cries out. "What you gonna do?"

Someone holding down his head giggles. "Old Meshikee, we're gonna fix you for the last time. You see that hill up there—the highest sandbank on the lake? Well, that's where you're going, Old Meshikee, 'cause we're gonna pitch you off the very top. And when you hit that water, you're gonna drop straight to the cold and deep! Drowned turtle, hee hee hee!"

"Oh, no!" cries Old Meshikee.

"Then you'll never play that big old drum again!"

Old Meshikee kicks and waves his arms, but it seems that the more he struggles, the more determined the Shagizenz are to carry out their plan. Eagerly, the Shagizenz drag him to the lip of the hill, where he can see nothing below but the beautiful lake itself. They snatch away their precious rope, and all begin to push.

"No!" cries Old Meshikee, and he seems to swoon, pulling his arms and legs, his head and tail inside his shell. But the Shagizenz give one mighty push, and over he goes, tumbling, tumbling down the great sandy hill, down toward the water, down toward the bottom of the lake.

SPLASH!

The Shagizenz are cheering. Some of them look carefully out over the lake where Old Meshikee has disappeared. No sign of Old Meshikee. Now he'll never play his silly old, noisy old, BIG old drum again!

All the way down the hill, the Shagizenz are singing and laughing and clapping their claws. Over and over they tell the story of how they got rid of Old Meshikee and his drum. They are so pleased with themselves. The afternoon quickly turns to evening, and of course the happy Shagizenz want most of all to bring out the drums and have a dance. Some of them start a fire, and some of them start to sing, and some of them put on their best moccasins and vests. What a party they are going to have, and best of all, there will be no Old Meshikee making noise on his big old drum.

Only some of the children are quiet, looking out over the water and thinking of the stories Old Meshikee told them.

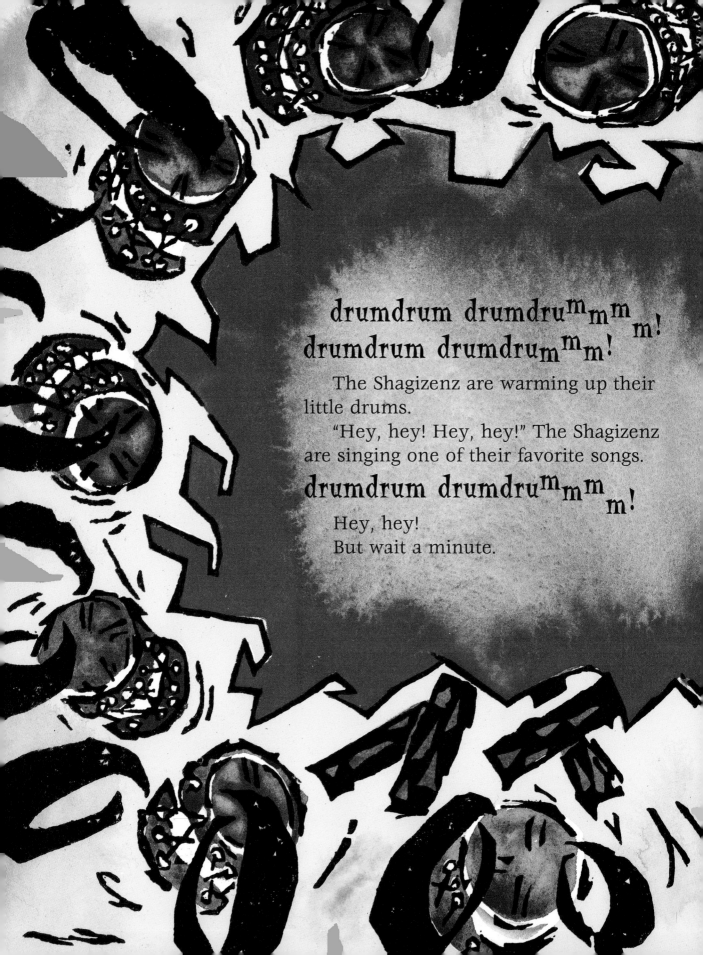

drumdrum drumdru^m^m^m_m!
drumdrum drumdru^m^mm! ^m!

The Shagizenz are warming up their little drums.

"Hey, hey! Hey, hey!" The Shagizenz are singing one of their favorite songs.

drumdrum drumdru^m^m^m_m!

Hey, hey!
But wait a minute.

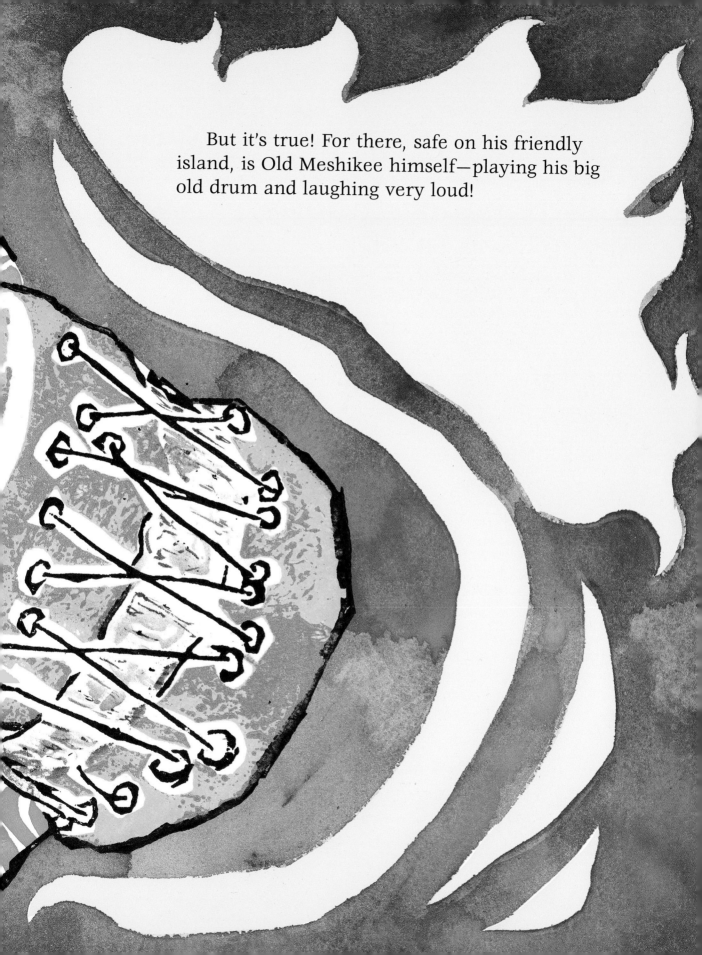

But it's true! For there, safe on his friendly island, is Old Meshikee himself—playing his big old drum and laughing very loud!

SOURCE NOTE

The Ojibwe* people, who live in the upper Great Lakes region of North America, have always respected the turtle as a wise, benevolent, and amusing animal. *Meshikee* is their word for "turtle," and in everyday usage it becomes a sort of proper name, like "Leo" or "Coyote" do in other cultures. This traditional story about Meshikee is one of many that Lolita Taylor learned from her Ojibwe grandfather as a child in the early 1900s. She told the story to my father in the 1930s and first told it to me in 1981.

"Old Meshikee and the Little Crabs" is similar to tales or fables that come from other cultures. In fact, the theme of "drowning" as punishment for a turtle appears frequently enough that folklorists have given it a name and number in their research indexes. It is interesting that around the world, Turtle is seen as a very clever fellow. He's not mischievous like a Trickster, but he shows a ready ingenuity that serves him as a survival skill. Beyond stories about Turtle himself, this tale also carries the familiar feel of popularized fables like "Br'er Rabbit and the Briar Patch," in which an innocent party tricks his enemies into releasing him.

There are several details in "Old Meshikee and the Little Crabs" that show you some tools or ways of doing things from the traditional life around the Great Lakes. For example, the rope, the baskets made of birch bark, and where to find firewood are all things that an Ojibwe grandmother or grandfather might mention when telling the story to children. Passing on details like these is part of how stories help to carry a culture from one generation to another.

As with any traditional story, the version that we are telling here is different in small ways from other versions you may have heard. We may spend a little more time on certain themes, or a little less on others, than another storyteller might. In fact, it might be a little different here from the way we've told it before. That's the way it is with stories: the body stays the same, but you can dress it in different clothes from time to time.

—Michael Spooner
Logan, Utah, 1996

*Also commonly spelled Ojibway, Ojibwa, or Chippewa. Anishinabe is an older name, which has been regaining usage lately, though some say it has a slightly different meaning and still isn't as widely known as these others. Frankly, we had a difficult time deciding which word to use.